The Baseball Player and the Walrus

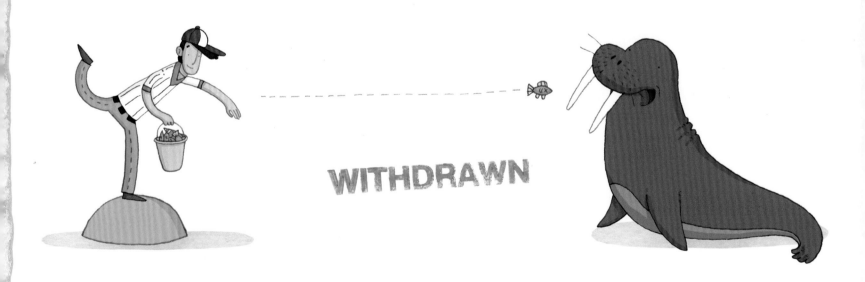

Ben Loory · illustrations by Alex Latimer

DIAL BOOKS FOR YOUNG READERS an imprint of Penguin Group (USA) LLC

For my father and the Brooklyn Dodgers.
With special thanks to Cecil Castellucci.
B.L.

For my dad
A.L.

DIAL BOOKS FOR YOUNG READERS
Published by the Penguin Group · Penguin Group (USA) LLC, 375 Hudson Street, New York, NY 10014

USA | Canada | UK | Ireland | Australia | New Zealand | India | South Africa | China | penguin.com

A PENGUIN RANDOM HOUSE COMPANY

Text copyright © 2015 by Ben Loory · Illustrations copyright © 2015 by Alex Latimer

Library of Congress Cataloging-in-Publication Data
Loory, Ben. · The baseball player and the walrus / by Ben Loory ; pictures by Alex Latimer. · pages cm
Summary: "A successful but unhappy baseball player finds companionship in the pet walrus he adopts but is soon faced with the great challenge of balancing his responsibilities and maintaining the costly upkeep of his new friend" —Provided by publisher. · ISBN 978-0-8037-3951-2 (hardcover) · [1. Baseball players—Fiction. 2. Walrus—Fiction. 3. Human-animal relationships—Fiction.] I. Latimer, Alex, illustrator. II. Title. · PZ7.L876324Bas 2015
[E]—dc23 2014002796

Manufactured in China on acid-free paper · 10 9 8 7 6 5 4 3 2 1
Designed by Jason Henry · Text set in Archer · The artwork for this book was created with scanned hand-drawn pencil lines which were then colored and textured on computer.

*O*nce there was a baseball player. He played in the major leagues, and made lots and lots and lots of money. People came from all around the world to see him play.

But the ballplayer was unhappy.
And no one knew why.

At night, the ballplayer would sit in his house—
or his hotel room, if his team was on the
road—and stare out the window into the night
sky and sigh.

"What's missing from my life?" he'd say.

Then one day the baseball player went to the zoo, and he saw all the animals. He saw the lions and the tigers and the giraffes and the elephants.

And then he came to the walrus.
"Wow!" said the baseball player. "That sure is some animal!"
And he stayed there all day long, just watching it.

And that night, as he lay in bed, he found himself laughing, remembering the walrus's antics.

BEST PLAYER

hehehe

It's so great the way the walrus lolls around, he thought.

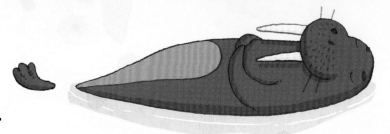

UURP! UURP!

And the way it makes those funny noises.

And I love when it gobbles down all of the fish, bobs its head around, and flaps its flippers!

And the baseball player decided right then and there that he was going to buy the walrus.

It turned out the walrus was very hard to buy. The zoo people didn't want to sell it. They were concerned that the baseball player wouldn't be able to take proper care of it.

But the baseball player was determined to prove them wrong. He built a special enclosure in his backyard for the walrus. It had a huge pool and plenty of places to lie out, and a retractable roof in case it got too cold or too hot. He bought lots of fish and barrels of walrus vitamins, and had fancy lights installed.

Basically, he showed the zoo people that he meant business.

And eventually, he brought the walrus home.

For a while, everything was absolutely wonderful.
The ballplayer spent all his time in the enclosure. He
petted the walrus and combed its mustache, told it stories

and taught it to play catch.

And the walrus was happy. It smiled and laughed all the time. And the ballplayer was happy, too.

In fact, the ballplayer was happier than he'd ever been in his life.

But then the baseball season started up again, and the ballplayer got very busy. There were practices and practices, and lots of away games, and he saw less and less of the walrus.

And as the baseball player sat in faraway hotel rooms, he got sadder and sadder by the day, thinking of the walrus sitting at home, with a lonely look on its face.

It was just too much for the ballplayer to bear.

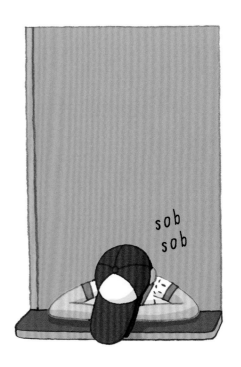

"I quit," he said to the team owner the very next day.

"What?" said the team owner.
"You can't quit!"
"I can, and I do," said the ballplayer.
"I miss my walrus. I'm going home."

And that was exactly what he did.

UURP!

But as it turned out—he hadn't noticed before—
it was very expensive to care for a walrus. Without a
job, it was hard for the ballplayer to afford the fish,
buy the vitamins, and maintain the whole enclosure.

The baseball player held out for as long as he could,
but eventually, he ran out of money. And on that day,
the zoo people came in a truck, and they loaded the
walrus back up.

"I'm sorry, walrus!" the ballplayer called after the truck. "I'll miss you! I already do! But I'll get you back! One day, I will! I'll do absolutely anything I have to!"

So, the very next morning the ballplayer got up, and he took a very deep breath. And he went to the stadium to see the owner of the team.

Home: 3

Visitors: 7

"I'm ready to play ball again," he said.

But it was too late. The team owner was mad.

"There's no place for you here," he said. "You should've thought of this before you quit. Your baseball-playing days are all over."

The ballplayer went home and sat and considered.

"I guess I'll have to get some other kind of job," he said.

He looked through all the jobs in the classified section.

"I'm not qualified for any of these," he sobbed.

In the morning the ballplayer walked slowly to the zoo.
I have to say good-bye to the walrus, he thought.

But when he got to the zoo he stopped—
there was a sign on the wall.

The ballplayer took the sign and ran to the zookeeper.
"I know exactly how to do this job!" he said. "Please
give me a chance! I won't let you down!"
"Okay," the zookeeper said.

And now, today, everything is fine. The baseball
player works at the zoo. He feeds the walrus fish and
makes sure it takes its vitamins.

He tells it stories and combs its mustache.

And sometimes, at night, the ballplayer turns on the lights, and he marks out a diamond on the field. And he gets out his old glove, and gives the walrus his cap, and the two of them play a little ball.